PUMPKIN PIE FOR SIGD

A Holiday Tale

By Jennifer Tzivia MacLeod • Illustrated by Denise Damanti

APPLES & HONEY PRESS

*With so much thanksgiving
for family near and far.*

—JTM

*To all the little things that will
someday become big.*

—DD

Sigd (SEE-gd or SEE-gid) is a Jewish holiday celebrated in Ethiopia fifty days after Yom Kippur. When Ethiopian Jews began coming to Israel, they brought the holiday with them, and in 2008, it was made an official Israeli national holiday.

Editorial Consultants:

Pnina Falego Agenyahu, Director of Interfaces and Synergy, Strategic and Planning Unit, Jewish Agency for Israel
Dr. Sharon Shalom, Chair, International Center for the Study of Ethiopian Jewry, Ono Academic College

The illustrations within were created using digital tools.

Apples & Honey Press
An imprint of Behrman House Publishers
Millburn, New Jersey 07041
www.applesandhoneypress.com
ISBN 978-1-68115-566-1
Text copyright © 2021 by Jennifer Tzivia MacLeod
Illustrations copyright © 2021 by Behrman House Publishers

Library of Congress Cataloging-in-Publication Data

Names: MacLeod, Jennifer Tzivia, author. | Damanti, Denise, illustrator.
Title: Pumpkin pie for Sigd : a holiday tale / by Jennifer Tzivia MacLeod ; illustrated by Denise Damanti.
Description: Millburn, New Jersey : Apples & Honey Press, an imprint of   Behrman House Publishers, [2021] | Audience: Grades K-1. | Summary: "An American immigrant to Israel misses Thanksgiving and is introduced to the holiday of Sigd"—Provided by publisher.
Identifiers: LCCN 2020017473 | ISBN 9781681155661 (hardback)
Subjects: CYAC: Sigd—Fiction. | Thanksgiving Day—Fiction. | Food—Fiction. | Immigrants—Israel—Fiction. | Israel—Fiction.
Classification: LCC PZ7.1.M246 Pu 2021 | DDC [E]—dc23
LC record available at https://lccn.loc.gov/2020017473

Design by Elynn Cohen
Edited by Ann D. Koffsky
Printed in China
1 3 5 7 9 8 6 4 2

1021/B1766/A6

"Can we make a pumpkin pie?" I ask my father. It's my first Thanksgiving since we moved to Israel from America, but Thanksgiving isn't a holiday here. Instead, my new friend Orly has invited me to celebrate Sigd with her family. It's a Jewish holiday from Ethiopia, where she was born.

I want to help make Orly's holiday special.
But I keep thinking about Thanksgiving: turkey,
stuffing, cranberry sauce. And family, especially
my baby cousin, Oliver, who's so far away. Can
it really be Thanksgiving so far from home?

"I don't know, Maddie," my father says.
"Where will we get a pumpkin?"
"What's a pumpkin?" Orly asks.
"Ohhh," she says, adding a
dash of color to my drawing.
Then, I have an idea.

We take our pumpkin pictures to Mrs. Ivanova, next door. Her family came here from Ukraine, and she's always trying to give us fruits and vegetables.

We don't speak Russian, and she doesn't speak Hebrew or English. But our pictures are good enough.

"Oh!" Mrs. Ivanova exclaims. She runs inside and comes back with . . .

"**Butternut squash**?" my father asks. "That could work. . . .We'll just have to bake it for a while first, to soften it up."

While the squash bakes, we find a recipe.

When the squash is ready, I mash it up with eggs, and Orly sprinkles in cinnamon. Then the recipe says to put in evaporated milk.

"Israel has almost everything we're used to, but I don't think they have evaporated milk here," my father says a little sadly.

Orly just shrugs. But I still want to try. The pumpkin picture worked with Mrs. Ivanova. And I know someone else who might be able to help.

Mr. Tautang answers the door slowly. His family just moved here from India. Orly and I hold up our new pictures. He puzzles over them, then shuffles inside and comes back with . . .

"**Coconut cream**?"
my father asks. "Sure,
that could work."

Orly stirs the coconut cream into the squash.
"What will you use for a crust?" my father asks.

"Leave it to us," I say.

Mrs. Calderon from Mexico scratches her head when she sees our pictures. Then her face lights up. "Aha!" she says. She darts inside and returns with something warm, all wrapped up. . . .

"**Tortillas**!" says my father.
"Maybe this will work after all."
 Our pie is ready just in time for
Orly's party.

Later, at Orly's apartment, we hand her mother the pie. She smiles and says, *"Melkam bahal."*

"That means 'happy holiday,'" says Orly.

Orly leads me through the crowd, stopping to kiss a few people while she looks for a spot where we can sit down. Suddenly, everybody gets up to greet a man in robes as white as coconut cream.

"Who's that man carrying the umbrella?" I whisper to Orly.
"He's a *kess*," she whispers back. "Our rabbi."
Everyone goes quiet as the kess stands up and says a blessing.

Then they're all crowding around the table, taking food and laughing, just like my aunts and uncles and cousins used to do on Thanksgiving, piling their plates high. "Save room for dessert!" they'd joke, patting their bellies.

Aunt Liora cried at the airport when we all said goodbye. And today, we're having Thanksgiving apart. I wonder if my baby cousin Oliver knows how to walk yet?

Orly points to something orange that looks a little like our mashed-up squash. "It's called *misir wat*," she says. "Spicy lentil stew. Extra delicious for Sigd."

Orly hands me a giant bubbly pancake. "*Injera*."

She dips hers in stew and gobbles it up. "You eat it with your hands."

But when I take a bite, instead of being sweet, like a pancake, the injera is sour. Not like a lemon, but like cheese.

"Interesting," I say. I put it down when Orly isn't looking. It's nothing like turkey and wild rice and cranberry sauce. Nothing here tastes like Thanksgiving.

Sometimes, America feels very far away.

Then I remember. "Want to try the pie?" I ask.

Before I can stop her, Orly grabs a spoon, scoops some out, and pops it in her mouth.

"Sweet!" she says in surprise. I scoop some too. I close my eyes, and there it is: the taste of home, right here in Israel. I can't help smiling.

When I open my eyes, I see that Orly has quietly put her plate down. She's taking a sip of water. "Interesting," she says politely. I start to giggle. She does too.

Orly brings me over to the kess and introduces me to him. "This is my friend Maddie from America. Today is her holiday too: Thanksgiving."

"Thanks-giving," he says. He smiles. "In Ethiopia, on Sigd, we used to pray to return to Jerusalem, to Israel. And now, Jews from all over the world are here together. Giving thanks."

The kess hands us each a piece of crumbly bread. "*Dabo,*" he says. "Bread for the holiday. Our holiday *and* yours."

The bread is warm and tastes a little of honey.
"*Melkam bahal*," says Orly. "Happy holiday."
"Happy Thanksgiving!" I say back.
And suddenly, it really does feel
like Thanksgiving. A special
Thanksgiving, with my favorite
flavors, the family I love . . .
and so many new friends!

A NOTE FOR FAMILIES

When I moved to Israel, my family and I lived in a *merkaz klita*, an immigrant absorption center for people from all over the world. There were people there from Mexico, India, Ukraine, Ethiopia, and Guatemala, and I loved meeting Jews from so many different cultures and traditions.

One thing I learned when I met Jews from Ethiopia is that the Jewish holiday of Sigd celebrates the day God first spoke to Moses at the burning bush. In Israel today, members of the Ethiopian community honor the day by fasting, reciting Psalms, and reading from the Torah. Afterwards, there is a festive meal with singing and dancing.

Israel has adopted Sigd as a national holiday, and since Sigd often falls very close to Thanksgiving, this story of a shared Thanksgiving/Sigd meal really could happen in Israel.

Sigd and Thanksgiving are perfect times to show our gratitude and think about all the good things in our lives.

What are *you* thankful for?

Have you ever been far away from someone you loved? What are some things you did, or could do next time, to stay connected to that person?

Welcoming people, like Orly does by inviting her new friend to her family's celebration, is also a Jewish value. How can you help make newcomers in your community feel welcome?

Happy reading,